Heir
of
Sorrows

Sylvie Krin

Heir
of
Sorrows

PENGUIN BOOKS
in association with
PRIVATE EYE

PENGUIN BOOKS

Published by the Penguin Group
27 Wrights Lane, London W8 5TZ, England
Viking Penguin Inc., 40 West 23rd Street, New York, New York 10010, USA
Penguin Books Australia Ltd, Ringwood, Victoria, Australia
Penguin Books Canada Ltd, 2801 John Street, Markham, Ontario, Canada L3R 1B4
Penguin Books (NZ) Ltd, 182–190 Wairau Road, Auckland 10, New Zealand

Penguin Books Ltd, Registered Offices: Harmondsworth, Middlesex, England

First published in Private Eye Productions 1987–8
Published in Penguin Books 1988

10 9 8 7 6 5 4 3 2 1

Filmset in Linotron 202 Palatino
Typeset, printed and bound in Great Britain by
Hazell Watson & Viney Limited
Member of BPCC plc
Aylesbury, Bucks, England

♛ *Chapter 1* ♛

The story so far: To the outward world theirs was the perfect marriage. They seemed to have everything – wealth, looks, a house in the country and two beautiful children. They were the envy of the world. But within the fragrant rose the green-eyed serpent of suspicion lay coiled waiting . . . waiting . . . waiting . . .

AS USUAL Charles rose early, put on his shot-silk monogrammed dressing-gown, drew back the curtains and looked across the rolling Gloucestershire wolds. In the August dawn, the trees and fields lay wrapped in the fine gauze of an early morning mist.

He took a deep breath and reflected on how peaceful the world could be. The words of his friend and mentor, Sir Laurens van der Post, came to him: 'All is one. All is harmony.' How very true that was.

But his reverie was disturbed by the sudden eruption of a throbbing bass sound from somewhere below. An unfinished watercolour of the Villa Toledo in Majorca trembled on its easel.

Instantly the calm of his morning vanished like the sun behind a cloud. 'Oh God,' he muttered, as he tightened his dressing-gown cord about him. 'Oh, God . . .'

♛ ♛ ♛

The scene that greeted him in the dining room was becoming familiar. Dancing on the table was the figure of his sister-in-law, the Duchess Fergiana, her red hair clashing violently with her cerise cowgirl outfit.

She clapped ecstatically to the sound of the record player and sang along: 'Wake me up before you go-go . . .'

The room was in semi-darkness, lit only by a strobe light fixed precariously to the crystal chandelier. In the gloom Charles could distinguish the figure of his brother Andrew slumped across the table, a half-filled glass of flat champagne at his elbow, his bow tie hanging loosely around his neck.

Some of the other faces were also known to him from the record sleeves in his wife's seemingly endless collection.

That one with the stubble . . . Colin someone? And the bald one who was something to do with football . . .

He tried to conceal his distaste as he watched them smoking and gyrating in a desultory manner on his parquet floor.

'Ahem . . .' he coughed. 'Has anyone seen my wife?'

Andrew stirred and opened one eye.

'All present and correct, sir,' he slurred, then fell back into a deep sleep.

A man in dark glasses and a slashed T-shirt ambled towards him. 'She went for a walk in the garden,' he drawled in an impeccable Etonian accent. 'She said she needed a breath of fresh air.'

'Do I know you?' stammered Charles.

'My father was at school with you,' the young man replied, taking a drag from a long cigarette and staring vacantly over Charles's shoulder. 'I say, where can a chap get some breakfast round here? I've been up all night and I'm starving.'

Charles didn't hear him. Already he was on his way out of the room, his heart pounding with unease.

👑   👑   👑

Charles sat dismally on his bed toying with his brushes. He had looked everywhere but Diana was nowhere to be found. His mind went back to the night before and the blazing row over the Madonna concert.

Diana had insisted that she should be free to do as she wished. He had taken his father's advice. 'You've got to put your foot down, my boy. We can't have her cavorting about with a load of doped-up weirdoes. It doesn't do the show any good.'

But she was young, beautiful and headstrong, like an untrained colt. 'I want to be free, d'you hear me?' She had screamed at him. 'Free. Free. Free!'

He got up wearily and started to trace the outline of a lone pine tree on the cliff's edge on his watercolour. He thought of a title for his work and he could see it in the Academy catalogue – *Despair* by A. C. Cartwright . . .

👑 *Chapter 2* 👑

Sensitive artistic Charles is finding married life difficult with the young headstrong Diana.

Almost half his age, she spurns his old-fashioned ways. He is at a loss to understand her world . . .

THE SUN shone fiercely from the cloudless blue Mediterranean sky. In the distance Charles could see Diana, dressed only in the scantiest of bikinis, her long, youthful limbs revealed. She lay languidly on a sun-lounger, her eyes closed and, as always, her Sony Walkman clamped about her ears.

Her tender pouting lips mouthed the now familiar lyric:
Sex is natural
Sex is good.
The sight of her sent a shudder down his spine.

He noted, too, that the copy of *The Innermost Voyage* by his friend and mentor, Sir Laurens van der Post – the book he had personally given to her for her holiday reading – lay discarded in the sand.

He had hoped that perhaps the wisdom of the wise old traveller would do something to bridge the ever-widening gap between them.

But clearly she preferred the brash music of pop singers to improving her mind.

Spain had been her idea – King Carlos's invitation to his sun-drenched palace in Majorca. He, Charles, would have preferred the silence of the Scottish moorland. The plaintive cry of the grouse, the purple heather stretching into the distance.

It was there, above all, he had discovered that a man could come to terms with the 'music of the inner self', as Sir Laurens had so movingly described it in his book *Mankind and the Lost Mystery*.

But Diana had been adamant.

'If you think I'm going to spend two weeks shut up in that dreary old castle with the rain pouring in, you're very much mistaken!'

He shuddered with distaste as he recalled the scene the night before they left.

'I've got to have sun. Everybody gets a tan in the summer. I'm not going to look all horrid and white!'

He remembered the slamming door. The car driving into the night. Whither he knew not . . .

His reverie was broken by the cheerful voice of his cousin the King.

'Buenas tardes, my old chum,' he cried, giving Charles a playful slap on the back. 'How you like everything? OK?'

He gestured towards Diana, lowering his voice. 'Such a beautiful young woman, your wife.' He nudged Charles in the ribs. 'You lucky man!'

Charles shifted uneasily in his deck-chair. Could the King only know his secret sorrow!

'Listen, amigo! Tonight we have a BEEG surprise! Just for you and the lovely Diana . . .'

Charles frowned, but did his best to show a polite anticipation.

'Another roast sucking pig?' he ventured.

The King laughed and slapped his thigh. 'Sucking pig, ha, ha, ha. You and your *Goon Show* jokes . . .'

👑   👑   👑

The Royal Palace of Los Trocaderos was ablaze with lights. In the huge banqueting chamber, all of Spain's ancient nobility had gathered to honour the royal visitors from England – the Duke and Duchess of Torremolinos, Don Pedro de Granada, the beautiful Marquesa del Monico. Everyone was there.

Suddenly the lights dimmed and the King beamed across to Charles. 'The surprise at last!'

There was an expectant hush followed by the plangent throbbing of guitars.

And then on to the spotlit floor stepped a slender figure dressed from head to toe in the black costume of the ancient Flamenco dancer.

'El Ferdinando heemself!' whispered the King. 'The greatest in all

Spain! His reputation as a dancer is matched only by his fame as a lover. Not for nothing do they call him the Matador of Broken Hearts!'

And then the music began . . . Quietly at first but building, building to a wild crescendo rich with all the torrid passion of this ancient people.

Charles's heart sank and he looked towards his wife. But her eyes were alight like a child at a pantomime.

As the castanets beat out their insistent primeval rhythm El Ferdinando moved inexorably towards Diana – a fragrant blood-red rose clenched between his strong white teeth.

Guitars, castanets, stamping feet reached a thrilling climax. Then suddenly – silence.

In one deft movement the Matador of Broken Hearts took the rose and placed it gently behind Diana's ear.

There was a gasp of surprise followed by a roar of rapturous applause.

'Olé! Olé! Viva El Ferdinando!'

♕   ♕   ♕

The clock struck midnight but there was no let-up for Charles as more and more of his distant relatives were led forward to shake his hand.

As he listened with half an ear to the whispered pleasantries of a charming old Contessa, he realized that he had not seen Diana since the end of the dance.

Then Carlos was at his side.

'Wasn't it just fantastic? What a fellow he is! What a rascal, eh? I have been looking for him everywhere to introduce you but' – he shrugged apologetically – 'he seems to have gone.'

Charles felt a cold chill in the warm Spanish night. He looked through the open window into the sweet smelling border below. Was it his imagination or could he hear the sound of familiar laughter from the ornamental lemon grove . . . ?

♛ *Chapter 3* ♛

*The future King of England longs to share with his young bride his deep
love of all things beautiful, but her thoughts, as ever, seem to be
somewhere else . . .*

THROUGH THE window of the chauffeur-driven limousine
Charles could see the craggy battlements and ancient towers of the
medieval city of Bayeux where his ancestors had once held sway.

How wonderful, he thought, that he should be returning to these
historic scenes – retracing what his friend and mentor, Sir Laurens van
der Post, had called 'Man's journey into the past'.

He could picture the wise old man at his side as they had walked
through the barren deserts of the Kalahari, explaining how time was
neither past nor future but a continuous web of dream and reality.

Eager to share his excitement Charles turned to Diana at his side.
'Isn't it tremendously exciting when . . .'

The words died on his lips as he realized that, as ever, she could not
hear him.

That infernal Walkman! 'Diana,' he shouted in a voice that made the
chauffeur turn uncomfortably, 'I am trying to talk to you!'

With a sulky pout she removed the offending headphones, which
continued to blare out the raucous strains of Michael Jackson's *Bad*.

With that one gesture Charles felt that they had grown more apart
than ever.

'We're nearly there, darling. I'm sure you're going to like the tapestry. Sir Hugh Casson tells me it changed his life completely! It's sort
of history coming alive.'

'More than can be said of some people I know,' she said, placing a
stick of low-cal menthol chewing-gum in her petulant mouth.

The barb stung like the arrow at the Battle of Hastings, and the car
sped on in silence down the long tree-lined avenue that led towards
the town.

Now the car slowed to negotiate the cobbled streets. A few weather-
beaten onion sellers paused in their daily tasks to salute their Royal
visitors.

'Salut vos Majestés!' cried one gnarled old veteran, his medals
proudly pinned to his bicycle.

Charles waved limply and noticed to his surprise that Diana had become more animated.

'Aren't they fabulous?' she cried. 'Can't we stop and have a look?'

His heart leapt. 'Arrêtez, Gaston,' he called through the glass partition, and the car drew up to the kerb. With one bound Diana sprang out clutching her bag and began to push her way through the citizenry towards the Pierre Cardin Boutique (London, Paris, New York, Abu Dhabi) on the corner of the Rue de Gaulle.

It was then he realized the bitter truth. He looked at his watch and muttered 'Damn'. He would have to do a face-saving royal walkabout whilst his immature young wife frittered away the nation's wealth.

*T*wo hours later, Charles left the Boulangerie, having heard far too much of the wartime memories of M. Balon, the *propriétaire* of *Les Deux Croissants*, Bayeux's *premier pâtisserie*.

Trying to keep his anger in check he strode through the door of Pierre Cardin.

To his amazement his wife was nowhere to be found and Monsieur Cardin himself came forward to greet him, rubbing his hands obsequiously.

'Have you seen my wife?' Charles demanded of the world-famous couturier.

'Mais oui, Monsieur, she is in ze changing room with young Marcel,' and even as he spoke the sound of giggling could be clearly heard from one of the cubicles.

Charles stepped forward and pulled back the curtain. There was Diana struggling into one of the great Parisian designer's latest creations in peach and beige taffeta, and at her side stood a handsome French youth with a moustache helping her with her zip.

Charles turned on his heel and walked heavily back to the car.

Suddenly the tapestry seemed as interesting as an old carpet discarded on an inner-city skip . . .

♛ *Chapter 4* ♛

A gulf is growing between them.

THE AUTUMN sunshine filtered through the tall windows of Kensington Palace. Charles looked out from his oak-panelled drawing room at the delightful vista of the leaves turning to gold in the park as nannies sedately wheeled their young charges towards the circular pond.

'What a delightful scene,' he mused. If only life were as peaceful for him. He could spend the whole morning capturing it in watercolours. Who knows? Perhaps it could even hang in next year's exhibition. *Ripeness Is All* by E. J. Arkwright . . .

The door opened and the royal equerry, Sir Alan Fitztightly, shimmered to his side.

Diana looked up from her copy of *The Face* and glanced appreciatively at the sky-blue knickerbockers of her husband's personal secretary.

'Beg pardon, Sir,' soothed Sir Alan in his impeccable Old-Etonian tones. 'Sir Laurens van der Post has just rung and has graciously accepted your invitation to dinner this evening.'

'Oh God, no!' exploded Diana, flinging the article on Terence Trent D'Arby petulantly on the floor. 'Why do we have to have that old bore? Why can't we have someone with a bit of zip?'

Charles bit his lip. 'Not in front of the servants,' he hissed through clenched teeth.

There was an awkward silence as Sir Alan, sensing that all was not well, bowed and walked backward out of the room. When he had gone Charles turned to his wife.

'Really, darling. I just don't understand you. How can you describe the world's most famous explorer a bore? He's a fascinating man who I personally find very exciting.'

'Well I hope you'll both be very happy!' she snapped. 'But I'm not just going to sit and listen to you two rabbiting on about bushmen and all that. Just you wait and see, I'll make your party go with a swing!'

*I*t was growing dark when Charles arrived back from his walkabout in the inner cities. It had gone well. The new Community Centre with its training facilities for the ethnic unemployed had impressed him greatly, particularly the young director Ron Stepney.

So engrossed had he been in a discussion on computer data processing that he had quite failed to notice how time was flying. And now he was late for his own dinner.

As he hurried along the hallway he could hear from the dining room the sound of conversation and laughter.

Relief surged through his body like sap rising in the flowers of spring. Diana was coping after all. His old friend and mentor and his difficult young wife had hit it off.

The door was suddenly flung open.

'Come on Charles. Where the hell have you been? Everyone's here!'

'What do you mean, everyone?'

'Well, you know – Mandy and Charlie Ricketson-Smythe, Bunty Coker, Georgie Cavendish – and Fergie and Andy, of course.'

As he walked in, his eyes took in an all too familiar scene. Ricketson-Smythe, his hair already dishevelled, was balancing a champagne bottle on his nose. It was an old trick which Charlie had witnessed many times. To his right a florid Bunty Coker was in the middle of one of his jokes, picked up in the City. An appreciative gaggle of débutantes hung on his every word.

With horror he saw in the midst of this appalling spectacle the wizened figure of Sir Laurens van der Post bent over his asparagus soup, his eyes glazed, his hand trembling with fury.

'. . . and then d'you know what happened?' cried Bunty Coker, waving his cigar in the sage's face. 'One of the coons got back in his car and shouted out "My one's a lot bigger than yours, whitey"!'

The whole company collapsed in convulsions of laughter. The Princess Fergiana was so overcome with mirth that she slapped Sir Laurens on the back causing him to expectorate a fragment of asparagus.

'Excuse me, Your Majesty,' said Sir Laurens, rising unsteadily to his feet. 'I am an old man and it is getting late. I think, if you don't mind, I'll make my excuses.'

'Of course.' Charles was at his side leading him mercifully towards the door.

In the hall, as he helped him on with his coat, he distinctly heard Georgie Cavendish's voice raised above the rest, 'And who in God's name was that old fart?'

Was he mistaken or was it the voice of Diana that replied, 'That was Charles, stupid.'

As their laughter rang through the palace, his dream lay shattered in a million fragments like the autumn leaves blowing in the cold evening air.

♕ *Chapter 5* ♕

Tension between the Royal Couple continues to grow. Despite his attempts to relax with homoeopathic meditation Charles's nerves are increasingly on edge.

CHARLES LEANT forward, brush in hand, and dabbed a smear of grey on his autumn landscape, *Ripeness Is All*. He would have to think seriously about changing the title, as the leaves had long begun to fall, spreading a carpet of gold on the frosted grass beneath. Even so, he felt pleased with his efforts and tomorrow he would show the canvas to Sir Hugh Casson, the most accomplished painter in the land. A smile of self-contentment played about his lips. Perhaps, after all, the consolation of Art could make up for his troubled heart.

Suddenly he became aware of a strange thumping sound in the corridor outside. 'Diana,' he called absently. 'Are you there?'

There was no answer, and the irregular noise continued, accompanied by bursts of high-spirited laughter.

'Probably disco-dancing,' he thought petulantly. 'She'll have that Walkman over her ears listening to . . .' He could never remember the names.

He got up from his chair but thought better of it and returned to his easel. The more he looked at his little picture, the better he liked it. It was true after all what Sir Laurens had said to him – 'The act of painting is merely holding a mirror to the inner creation.'

Bonk! Bonk! Bonk!

What was that noise? It really was too much. He strode purposefully towards the door and opened it. Charles was greeted by a tennis ball which hit him smack on the forehead.

'Ace!' laughed his wife delightedly. Charles rubbed his forehead in disbelief. Diana was standing at one end of the corridor in the scantiest of tennis skirts, holding a racket in one hand.

He was reminded of the poster of the young tennis player pinned up in pride of place above his mantelpiece when he was a student in Trinity Hall. For a moment, seeing her like that, a wave of nostalgia mingled with desire flooded over him as he remembered their early days of courtship.

But who was the tanned muscular figure at her side, dressed in

white shorts and a T-shirt bearing the slogan 'Tennis players do it with a racket'?

Diana picked up another tennis ball and threw it playfully at the young man standing next to her.

'This is Rod,' she giggled. 'Rod. Charles. Charles. Rod.'

'Hi Chuck. Just helping the missus with her service.' He grinned. 'She's coming along a treat. She'll be just great on the day.'

Charles flushed. 'What is this Diana?' he demanded.

'It's a charity tennis match. I told you but you weren't listening. You were doing your silly picture.'

Charles's blood rose to his ears. 'You are not playing in any tennis match. Not dressed like that.'

'Come on, cobber, don't be a square,' ventured the athletic Australian tennis coach.

'Do you realize who you're talking to?'

'Oh, Charles,' snapped Diana. 'Don't be so bloody pompous!' Flinging her Dunlop Maxply to the floor, she flounced into her bedroom, leaving an uncomfortable heir to the throne face to face with a bemused Rod McGargle.

When Charles awoke the following morning he was in good spirits. His father had been right. It had been necessary to put his foot down and show Diana who was boss. She was still a child, he told himself, and she needed authority as well as love.

Putting on his dressing-gown, he sat down to his daily breakfast of wholemeal prunes and live Bulgarian natural yoghurt.

'The papers, Sire,' announced Sir Alan Fitztightly, bringing in freshly ironed copies of the morning papers on a silver salver.

On top of the pile, in lurid colour, was a picture of Diana looking no better than a Page 3 girl, revealing to all the world what he believed should be for a husband alone to see.

'Princess Thigh!' screamed a huge headline in the *Star*. 'What Lovely Legs, Ma'am,' said *The Times*. 'Princess Takes Part in Charity Event,' said the *Independent*. There was no escaping it. He had failed.

The phone rang ominously, and instinctively he knew who it was. The voice of his father exploded at the other end.

Charles's heart sank, and once again he was a little boy at the gates of Gordonstoun. Would it never be any other way?

♛ *Chapter 6* ♛

*R*umours about the marriage of Charles and his young bride Diana have burgeoned and the ripples have spread as far as Windsor Castle.

'*E*NTER!' BARKED the familiar naval tones of the Duke of Edinburgh. Charles felt the years roll back, and he was once again waiting outside the study of Dr Kurt Ribbentrop, the legendary Headmaster of Gordonstoun.

As he nervously pushed open the oak-panelled door he found his father standing with his back to the blazing log fire. In front of him, spread out on the exquisitely carved Sheraton coffee table, lay a garish spread of the morning's newspapers.

There, in crude contrast to the elegance of the Fabergé carpet and a quietly ticking Ormolu carriage clock on the mantelshelf, was the reason for his summons.

'Di's Been Chucked!' cried one.

'Di's Disco Rentboy,' echoed another.

'Are They Heading for the Rocks?' asked yet another.

Philip picked up one of the offending tabloids and brandished it in his son's reddening face.

'This has gone far enough!' he bellowed, as if tearing a strip off some naval rating who had been caught asleep on the Watch.

Charles felt helpless, as he always did. He hated these moments of confrontation. Desperately he groped in his mind for the advice of Sir Laurens.

'In moments of stress be still and build a bridge over troubled waters,' he had said, but it seemed of little avail as the Duke continued on his tirade.

'Your mother is very upset. And as for granny – well she's hardly getting any younger is she? We've worked bloody hard to keep this show on the road and now you're letting us all down, d'you hear?'

The words stung Charles like the lash of a whip. 'I . . . er . . . terribly . . .' he began. But the Duke was in no mood to listen.

'It's up to you, boy, to bring her to heel before we end up as the laughing stock of Europe!'

Charles searched desperately for some way to defend his beautiful bride, but he knew in his heart of hearts that there was an awful truth in what his father had said.

*I*t's absolutely terrible,' said Charles sympathetically as he peered at the remnants of Mrs Cadwallader-Llewellyn's front room, devastated by the flood waters that had swept through South Wales in the wake of the hurricane.

It had been a good idea of granny's for them both to visit the disaster area together and see, as he put it, how the community were coping in the post-hurricane deprivation situation.

There was no doubt that a Royal visit could lift morale amongst the general populace. He said as much to the handsome young subaltern who was rowing them down Carmarthen High Street, Captain Hemple-Rupertson of the Powys Grenadier Guards, drafted in on this occasion to assist the civil power in their hour of need.

'You bet, Sir,' he agreed with a grin that showed a dazzling set of white teeth as he pulled hard on the oars, his muscles rippling under his spotless scarlet tunic.

Charles turned to Diana to see how she was coping with the scenes of desolation in his beloved Wales.

'Look darling, there's the church where they've set up the emergency soup kitchen. Isn't that amazing?'

But she seemed not to hear, preoccupied by something beyond his ken.

The boat drew in to the improvised gangplank and Charles jumped expertly ashore and began to shake hands with the reception committee, practising his few words of Welsh learnt long ago at the time of his investiture.

'Ich bin ein eisteddfodd nicht wahr,' he said to a curtseying Mayoress and worked his way down the line of dignitaries.

At the end of the row the Mayor himself grasped his hand warmly. 'Good of you to come, Sir, considering all the trouble at home and everything. So sorry to see that your wife couldn't be with you.'

Charles flushed. 'What d'you mean?' he flared. 'My wife is . . .'

He turned and, true enough, she was not beside him as he had imagined. Instead he could just see in the distance the little boat being firmly propelled by Captain Hemple-Rupertson towards the improvised disco on the roof of the multi-storey carpark.

Spots of rain began to fall and Charles felt his hopes being washed away like so much debris in the swollen flood-water of the river . . .

♛ *Chapter 7* ♛

*P*ress speculation concerning the marriage has reached fever pitch and there have even been questions in the House.

CHARLES CAREFULLY undid his bow tie and smiled at his reflection in the ornate Ludwig II baroque mirror. For the first time in what seemed for ever he felt a measure of contentment. What his friend and mentor, Sir Laurens van der Post, had once called 'a settling of the waters on the inner lake'.

He cast his mind back over the events of the last three days.

First there was the triumphant arrival at Berlin airport – the cheering crowds of Burgermeisters clad in traditional lederhosen, waving their feathered hats and shouting 'Guten Abend, Mein Führer! Wilkommen am Deutschland! Sieg Heil!'

Then the walkabout in the autumn sunshine with flaxen-haired smiling children pressing garlands of freshly picked edelweiss into Diana's hands.

And how well she had behaved from the very start! From the moment she had stepped off the plane and touched his hand reassuringly as the band had struck up *Deutschland Über Alles*. It was a tiny gesture, but it meant so much. Even the press had noticed. 'The Reconciliation!' they had all cried the following morning. 'Princess of Smiles!', 'Happy Di's Are Here Again!'

And so they were. He looked again at the figure staring back at him in the mirror. Diana's new tenderness was acting like an elixir of youth. At nearly 40 he wasn't looking so bad after all. But the question nagged at him: 'Why the sudden change?'

Staying with their cousins Willie and Tufti Van Holstenpilsner-Lager had been a joy. Diana had been politeness itself, even applauding at the Wild Boar Hunt at midnight. Gone was the Walkman, the sullen silence and the provocative pout.

At Cologne cathedral he had really felt that they had shared the experience together, as the warm autumn sunlight filtered through the stained glass window on to her soft, peach-like cheeks.

Her eyes had shone as Dr Vorsprung Durch-Technik had explained the intricate skills of the restorer. Could it be, he wondered, that the fragile fabric of their marriage was itself being restored?

And there had been moments of levity, too, at the Grosserbeerguten Lager factory, when he had urged her to sup the classic Bavarian brew they called 'the water of the Gods'. How they had laughed when his blushing Diana had for a moment sported a Dickie Davies-style moustache of foam!

And, to cap it all, there was the magic of a night at the opera. The immortal melodies of Wolfgang Mozart had flowed over them like a healing balm. How appropriate! *The Marriage of Figaro* . . .

♛   ♛   ♛

*I*n the baronial hall below where the portraits of his ancestors hung
in solemn ranks on the oak-panelled walls, the grandfather clock
struck midnight. Charles took a man-sized, monogrammed tissue and
wiped a bead of perspiration from his brow.

He looked for the waste-paper basket and saw it in the corner. But
wait! What was lying there at the bottom? On a screwed-up sheet of
notepaper he recognized the familiar handwriting of his father.

Fear struck him, but curiosity compelled him to pick it up and
smooth out the note on the dressing table.

His heart beat like a hammer as he read:

> Dear Diana. We've talked it over and this is it. You can do what you bloody well like in your spare time but when you're on parade showing the flag you bloody well behave yourself and make it look good!
>
> Keep smiling and pretend you're enjoying yourself. That's what you're paid for.
>
> If there's any more trouble from you, my girl, you'll be out on your ear!
>
> > *PHILIP,*
> > *Duke of Edinburgh.*

Charles slumped on to the bed lifeless – his world no more than a crumpled tissue of dreams . . .

♕ *Chapter 8* ♕

Charles is exploring every avenue to bring about a reconciliation.

THE ANCIENT medieval clock of Clarence House struck four and as the last stroke died on the air the palace sentries, in their cherry red tunics, performed the ancient ritual of change of Watch.

A grey autumn mist settled over St James's Park as lights were switched on in nearby offices and hotels. Charles helped himself to another cucumber sandwich from the silver salver. He felt reassured by the thought that there were some things in life that never changed.

'Another drop of gin in your tea, dear?' inquired his grandmother.

Her radiant smile reinforced his new-found sense of stability. It was truly amazing, he thought to himself, how at the age of 87 this wonderful woman was able to dispense wisdom as freely as she did her Gordon's. The words of his friend and mentor, Sir Laurens van der Post, came to mind: 'The wisdom of the old is like the oak tree. The older it gets the more people shelter under its boughs.'

'What your grandfather and I used to do,' she said, diverting her eyes for a moment from the flickering of the television screen, where the results of the 3.30 at Sedgemore Park were being announced: first, *Dirty Digger* 3-1, second, *Nancy Boy* 7-4, third, *Bob's-A-Flop* 100-1 favourite.

'What was I saying, dear?'

'About you and grandpa.'

'Oh, yes. There's nothing we enjoyed better than a good laugh and a good night out together. He loved the Crazy Gang. I don't suppose you remember them?'

Charles thought hard. Alas, no. It was more *The Goons* and *Monty Python* in his day.

'Margaret was saying that there's a very amusing Australian who dresses up as a lady. I'm sure you and Diana would enjoy it.'

Charles swallowed the last drop of his gin-flavoured Earl Grey. Yes, he thought, once again granny had come up trumps! He would get Fitzalantightly to arrange for tickets.

The last notes of the National Anthem faded and the house lights dimmed. There was an expectant rustle as the huge audience of celebrities prepared themselves for the entertainment ahead.

Charles glanced in the half light at his young wife. Her eyes shone with delight and she leant forward like a small girl at a panto as the band struck up a ragged version of 'Waltzing Matilda'.

The curtain parted and on to the stage staggered what Charles could only imagine was an underprivileged tramp from the inner cities. But as soon as he greeted the audience with a vile belch and a cry of 'Hello, you dirty pommy bastards!' Charles knew at once that he was Australian.

For a moment he felt a kinship with this rude colonial. He had met many such colourful figures during his walkabouts in Dempster's Creek and other faraway locations.

He was about to mention this to Diana when his eye was caught by what appeared to be a snake in the trousers of the figure on the stage, who was introducing himself as Sir Les Paterson, Australia's Cultural Attaché.

GARY ANDREWS 1987.—

There could be little doubt as to the nature of this giant appendage and the heir to the throne felt a shudder of distaste.

Sir Les then took a swig at a bottle and remarked, 'I mustn't overdo the amber nectar or my one-eyed trouser snake will go to sleep!'

To Charles's intense dismay the Princess of Wales squealed with laughter, clutched him by the arm and cried delightedly, 'Darling, isn't he an absolute hoot?'

♛   ♛   ♛

*T*he show lasted for what seemed an eternity. More than once
Charles had felt a compelling urge to leave the theatre rather than
listen to the barrage of filth, but he was prevented by confusion at his
wife's obvious pleasure in each successive crescendo of crudity.

Afterwards she insisted that they should go backstage to congratulate the perpetrator of the outrage and as they entered the crowded
dressing room he asked her not to be too long. He was already feeling
oppressed and alienated by the gushing showbiz atmosphere so
beloved of his brother Edward.

'Darling, darling, you were wonderful!' chorused a throng of tux-
edoed first-nighters, as they pressed forward to congratulate the great
Australian. Then, to his horror, Charles saw Diana herself approach
the star and warmly embrace him. 'You were terrific! I loved that song
about you and your donger. Do you know the one Fergie told me
about the West Indian nudist who had his nuts eaten by . . . er . . . I
think it was a squirrel, actually. It was so funny! Bunty Coker and
Charlie Ricketson-Smythe nearly had a heart attack!'

👑　　　👑　　　👑

*S*tanding in the cold by the stage door Charles looked at his watch.
It was midnight but still her laughter rang out from the dressing
room above him – a laughter he could not share.

Outside in the rain-spattered street a homeless wanderer rummaged
through the dustbins. They were both, in their own way, searching,
searching, searching . . .

♛ *Chapter 9* ♛

The heir to the throne seems to have grown further and further apart from his young bride. They appear to have no interests in common. Yet now there is a glimmer of hope on the horizon.

THERE WAS a discreet knock on the door of Charles's study and his equerry, Sir Alan Fitztightly, coughed quietly to announce his presence.

'There is a Mr Ronald Stepney and his assistant to see you, Sire. I believe they have brought your speech for this evening.'

Charles beamed. He was always pleased to see the enthusiastic young man who had provided so much hope for the people in the inner cities.

He put down his signed copy of Sir Hugh Casson's *Interesting Buildings of Gwent* with its exquisite little illustrations in watercolour by the author.

'Good morning, Your Highness. I trust this draft will please you, although you must of course feel free to put in your own personal touches.'

Charles took the packet and quickly scanned the typewritten pages. He particularly liked the beginning: 'Ladies and gentlemen of the architectural profession, it is a tremendous privilege to address you this evening in this historic setting.'

It improved the more he read, phrases leaping out at him in their brilliance: 'Hideous monstrosities . . . Lack of planning . . . Grotesque irresponsibility . . . Ghastly glass gulags . . .'

The architect hovered expectantly at Charles's shoulder.

'This is terrifically good. You and Mr Knevitt are to be congratulated. This will really set the cat among the pigeons!'

Charles felt a surge of excitement. What a pity that Diana was not going to be there to hear him. Never mind. He could tell her about it in the morning.

What was that image again? 'Skyscrapers standing around like the Harlem Globetrotters!' Brilliant . . . absolutely brilliant.

♛   ♛   ♛

*T*he thin morning sun filtered wanly through the leaded window of the breakfast room of Kensington Palace. Outside commuters bustled on their way to work, their heads buried in newspapers reminding him of a phrase of his friend and mentor, Sir Laurens van der Post: 'The foolish bustle like ants, but only the wise man journeys inward on the voyage of self-discovery.'

The papers were spread out on the table amongst the exquisite Meissen porcelain. As he picked up one after the other, the front pages told of the success of his speech. The coverage was truly amazing. Not since the 'carbuncle' episode had he achieved anything like this impact.

Gone was the image of the mystic wimp talking to his flowers, in its place a hard-hitting modern prince, a social commentator and a man to be reckoned with.

'Listen to this, darling,' he said, reading out a long editorial from the *Independent*.

' "There can be no doubt that Prince Charles speaks for millions when he voices his profound disquiet at the state of modern . . ." '

'Great. Fantastic,' chimed in Diana, as he continued for several min-
utes to intone the words of Sir William Rees-Mogg.

'Say what you like about the press,' he concluded, 'there are times
when they get it right.'

'Oh, yah,' agreed Diana. 'Absolutely.'

Charles basked in the warm glow of his young wife's approbation.
There could be no doubt, he thought, as he poured himself a second
cup of Old Mother Booker's Breakfast Blend Tea, that at last she had
seen the man he believed himself to be – the crusader with the reticent
shell.

He suddenly noticed that although there was a copy of the *Sun* with
the headline: 'Good Old Charlie!' open in front of Diana, her attention
was focused on an advertisement in the *Tatler* magazine. Out of the
corner of his eye he espied the words: 'Come to Whacky Manhattan
for the Christmas Experience You'll Never Forget.'

'Look,' she cried. 'Isn't this just too amazing?'

'What's that, darling?'

'Look at this skyline. Isn't it a fantastic sight? Empire State Building,
the World Trade Center . . . Fergie's been and she says when you get
to the top it's another world. Charlie Ricketson-Smythe was sick in the
lift half-way up the Chrysler Building. He was pissed, as usual . . .
and Bunty Coker says he could swing us an invite to Studio 54.'

'But mummy's expecting us at Windsor. You know that perfectly
well,' he protested.

'Well, you can go to grotty old Windsor if you like. I'm going where
the action is! We're going to hit the Big Apple.'

With that she furiously threw down her copy of the glossy magazine, smashing the priceless porcelain teapot.

Charles watched in despair as a torrent of tepid tea engulfed the
newspapers like an ominous primeval stain . . .

♛ *Chapter 10* ♛

It is Christmas but will it be a season of goodwill for the troubled heir to the throne and his beautiful young consort?

THE SNOW was falling heavily over Windsor Great Park. The few trembling deer sheltered under the gnarled oak tree as the sharp winter sun turned a blood-red as it sank majestically behind the M4.

Charles drew the curtains and switched on the light. He was alone and had a welcome opportunity to wrap his presents, especially his gift for Diana.

He picked up the framed watercolour of St Paul's as it had once been, before the forest of skyscrapers had marred its noble outline. It was all his own work, and even Sir Hugh Casson himself had complimented Charles on its subtle colouring and economic use of line.

Charles had enjoyed his afternoon at the workshop of Jeremiah Bulstrode, By Appointment Picture Framer to the Royal Household. A thrill had run through his whole being as the venerable craftsman had picked his framed work from a rack where it had stood alongside the immortal masterpieces of Van der Toblerone and Butoni the Younger.

He selected a sheet of coloured paper and wrapped it lovingly around the picture. Then he inscribed the tag 'Diana from Charles', and took it into the Great Hall where the towering 600-foot Norwegian spruce stood bedecked with glittering baubles as it had done since the days of Prince Albert.

He hoped it would give her the same pleasure that it had given him . . .

♛   ♛   ♛

The mighty Windsor sun-clock thundered the half-hour and Her Majesty the Queen pulled her familiar fur-coat around her shoulders.

'Are we ready?' she inquired, addressing the assembly in the porch. 'You know the Dean likes us to be punctual for the midnight service.'

Her regal eye surveyed the family as they stood expectantly in the

- GARY ANDREWS 1987 -

candlelight. The Duke of Edinburgh began his customary head count.
'One, two, three, four . . .' he barked in his nautical tone. 'Bloody hell!
We're one chap short! I might have known it! Where is she, boy?'

Charles winced and tried to remember where Diana had been last
seen. Was she upstairs watching *Blind Date* or was she in the bath with
that Walkman listening to . . . who was it now? 'Pepsi and Shirley'
they were called were they not . . .?

'I . . . er . . .' he stammered as his father tapped his foot
impatiently.

'We can't stand here all night. Your mother'll get the bloody flu!'

Then, as he spoke, the Duke's voice was drowned by the sound of
car engines accelerating into the courtyard. The family were blinded

by the flash of headlights swinging across their faces and deafened by the screeching of brakes against gravel.

The car doors opened to let out the blast of disco music from the stereo and then out leapt Diana, her face flushed, her eyes wild with excitement.

'Wow!' she exclaimed. 'We made it just on time. Bunty did a ton in the fast lane all the way down! It was such a laugh.'

From the white BMW the said Bunty Coker clambered out in full evening dress followed by the familiar figures of Charlie Ricketson-Smythe and Georgie Cavendish, who was holding a Harrods' bag crammed with clinking bottles.

Charles and his family were mesmerized by this sudden invasion.

'Where do we stash the booze, Di-sie?' asked Georgie, lighting herself a cigarette and sticking the match in Charlie Ricketson-Smythe's ear.

'Shove it on the floor by the tree and get a move on,' replied Diana.

'Yah. I know – opening time's 12 o'clock. Ha ha!' chimed Ricketson-Smythe as he followed Georgie inside with a large Fortnum's hamper in his arms.

The Royal party, still stunned at the unexpected intrusion, began to move silently towards the chapel where already the Reverend Maclean stood sycophantically under the lych-gate waiting to welcome his Royal guests.

As their feet padded on the snow Charles heard the crunch of breaking glass and a loud oath.

'Oh, damn!' cried Ricketson-Smythe. 'I seem to have put my foot in it, whatever it was. Looks like some sort of picture-thing. God, I'm so sorry!'

Charles lowered his head as he shuffled towards the welcoming canon. So many shattered fragments, so many broken dreams . . .

♛ *Chapter 11* ♛

As the New Year bells are about to ring out, Charles resolves to make 1988 a year of reconciliation.

THE TALL trees of the Sandringham Estate stood silhouetted against an unusually bright winter sky. Charles crunched the bracken underfoot as he walked disconsolately behind the main shooting party.

Ahead of him he could hear the distinct rasp of his father as he barked orders to all and sundry. 'Mine!' he bellowed, and Charles heard the sharp retort of the Duke's handmade nineteenth-century Underberg twelve-bore as it brought down a brace of barn-owls.

Charles shuddered inwardly and stopped to sit down on a mossy log, a victim of the October storm. He put down his own Purdey, a gift from the Sultan Mohammed Bin-Liner during Charles and Diana's state visit to his desert kingdom some years before.

How happy they had been then! In the cold December afternoon, Charles was suddenly warmed by the memories of those distant times: Diana girlishly applauding the famous camel dancing, and blushing demurely as Fatima, the royal belly-dancer, sensuously popped a sugared sheep's eye into Charles's mouth.

BANG! BANG! He was brought down to earth by his father's distant shout: 'Hedgehog! Got him! 'Course it's fair game, Perkins! Pick it up and bake it!'

Charles sat silent and let the party drift out of sight.

It was getting late, soon it would be New Year's Eve, *Auld Lang Syne* and that familiar sinking feeling of another directionless year gone by. But, above all, it was the year when the nagging rift between him and his young bride had seemed to grow ever wider.

Yes! This year would be different. He resolved then and there to abandon his pride, his reserve, and go to her – to meet her half-way at least.

The words of his old friend and mentor, Sir Laurens van der Post, came to him as the sun dipped behind the craggy turrets of Sandringham Castle. 'When a man builds a bridge, he must first decide on which side he intends to begin.'

*U*pstairs Charles was changing for the festivities ahead, not into his customary grey suit, but into a box-shouldered Jacobo Yamani designer jacket with matching Tim Smith baggy trousers and leather 'Princeton' loafers borrowed for the occasion from his brother, Edward.

It was all going to plan. A new image, a new look for the New Year.

No longer could she dismiss him as a fusty old fogey. How did his brother put it? 'You could be Jonathan Ross's younger brother.'

Still, he felt a twinge of unease at not wearing a tie and having deliberately omitted to shave. But it would all be worth it, he told

himself, as he donned a baseball cap with a built-in FM stereo tuner.

In the room below he could hear the party in full swing, distinguishing Diana's laughter above the droning voice of Charlie Ricketson-Smythe and the giggling of Georgie Cavendish. And was that Bunty Coker singing along to 'So Here It Is, Merry Christmas . . .'?

With his New Year resolution intact he made his calculated entrance. One minute to twelve. He would show them!

He thrust open the door and suddenly all eyes were on him.

The expressions of stunned incredulity gave way to barely suppressed sniggering, followed by a gale of hysterical laughter.

'Brilliant joke, Charles!' guffawed Ricketson-Smythe, spilling his glass of champagne all over Georgie Cavendish's head.

Charles blushed. 'I've no idea what you mean,' he said with as much conviction as he could muster.

'The clobber, old man!' shrieked Ricketson-Smythe. 'It's not fancy dress, you know.'

Charles looked at Diana for comfort. Surely she would appreciate his attempts at a new youthful look?

The icy expression in her eyes told him another story entirely . . .

As the bells rang out and the assembly linked arms and began to sing the traditional song . . . 'Should auld acquaintance be forgot . . .' the word *auld* was the only word he could hear . . . *auld . . . auld . . . auld . . .*

♛ *Chapter 12* ♛

*W*inter has settled over Highgrove. Short days and long nights add to Charles's deepening sense of frustration.

DAME WINTER had cloaked the stately trees of the park with her icy grip. A small bushy-tailed squirrel darted out across Charles's path as he wandered aimlessly down Mountbatten Walk. How purposeful the small creature seemed in his quest for nuts. How this contrasted with his own meandering footsteps as his Wellingtons crunched the ice-laden worsnip and gaythorne on the verges beneath his feet.

The clatter of horse's hoofs roused him from his reverie. 'Get out of the way, you bloody oaf!' barked a woman's voice. He recognized it from her appearances on television, particularly the one Diana liked – *A Question of Sport*, with the man in the sweater. It was his sister, riding out on her chestnut gelding, Twisker, from her neighbouring estate of Gatcombe Park.

'Sorry, Charles. I thought you were some idiot trying to get himself killed.'

Charles smiled nervously. Even though she was some years his junior she had always made him feel inadequate somehow, her force-fulness and strength of character reminding him in many ways of their father.

'I'm off to Africa next week. What are you up to? Nothing much by the look of it.'

Charles blushed.

'About time you pulled your finger out and did something useful.'

Although he knew it was futile, Charles again tried to explain his feelings about his life to his sister. He searched his mind to recall the words of his friend and mentor, Sir Laurens van der Post. 'Some are called to go into the desert, others to sit at home by the fire and look at the embers.'

Anne snorted and wheeled her mount back towards him. 'You do talk twaddle sometimes, Charles. You can't spend your whole life gazing at your navel. You'll earn no one's respect that way, least of all that Diana girl you married.' So saying she spurred Twisker onward and, delivering a confident slap on the horse's rump with her whip, Anne galloped off into the morning mist.

Her words, however, remained and stung him like a swarm of angry hornets . . .

'*O*h there you are.' Diana was sitting in the drawing room with her feet up on the sixteenth-century Weinstock *chaise-longue*. She was simultaneously reading *Smash Hits* magazine and watching the Mercantile Snooker Classic on the television.

'What have you been up to?'

Normally his response would have been muted, perhaps a 'nothing much' or a 'you know, dear', but on the long trudge home against the darkening winter sky and the mournful cry of the solitary peewit he had thought long and hard about his sister's admonition.

As he had climbed the old moss-covered stile at the bottom of Bowes-Lyon Meadow he had resolved to take a leaf out of Anne's book.

Charles strode towards the television and manfully turned it off just as the commentator whispered: 'It's a free ball and Steve's elected to take the brown.' Diana looked startled. She was about to object, but Charles spoke quickly.

'I've been thinking . . . er . . . There's a lot to be done you know . . . things to do . . . that sort of thing . . . like Anne you see . . . she's always on the go . . . travelling the world.'

Diana gazed at him.

'You mean like abroad?' she asked.

'Yes, that's it. You've got the picture,' he replied enthusiastically. 'We'll both go and show them all, you and me, that we really you know mean business . . . together.'

Her face lit up. It was an expression he had almost believed he would never see again.

'D'you really mean it, Charles?'

'I've never meant anything so much in all my life.'

She jumped up and hugged him.

'Oh, Charles, you're wonderful. That means we can join Fergie and the gang in Klosters. Great! Great! Great! Gluhwein here we go-go!'

Charles suddenly saw in his mind's eye a tiny man on skis being engulfed by a huge white avalanche burying him deep . . . deep . . . deep . . .

👑 *Chapter 13* 👑

*H*is Royal Highness the Prince of Wales is marking the 200th anniversary of Australia. But would his own relationship last as long?

'WOW! Have you ever seen anything like it?' Diana tugged at Charles's arm, drawing him to the edge of Sydney Harbour.

And indeed the spectacle was truly awesome. As far as the eye could see, ships of every size and shape bobbed happily on the glistening azure waters of the ancient harbour. Flags of many nations fluttered proudly, proclaiming their anniversary tribute. At the centre of it all the majestic tall ships lay anchored, a reminder of the first settlers under the intrepid Captain Cook, who had claimed the new territory for the British Crown when he sailed into Patterson Bay in 1788.

But were they the first settlers? Charles's sense of uneasiness marred the high spirits of the moment, and he recalled his famous walk through the Kalahari with his friend and mentor, Sir Laurens van der Post. The eyes of the wise old man had filled with tears as he told the tragic story of the aboriginal people of Australia. These proud tribesmen who understood the ways of the stars and the songs of the

moon. Men who could find their way through the trackless desert with nothing more than an unconscious race memory that had existed for millions of years.

And now they were the exploited victims of the white man's greed, shunned and despised by the invaders of their homeland. How had Sir Laurens put it? 'The great white eagle feels no mercy towards the trembling mole.'

He had tried to capture some of what he felt in the speech he had made in front of the Opera House, and he vowed the very next day to go on a pilgrimage to Boolabanga Rock to see for himself the mysteries of these once-great people.

♕   ♕   ♕

At last the Land Rover came to a shuddering halt as the sun beat down relentlessly on the blood-red plains of Murdoch Ridge. Ahead stood the huge outcrop of Boolabanga Rock, the mystical centre regarded by the aboriginals as the sacred source of 'the dreaming power'.

'It really is tremendous, darling. You feel sort of drawn in in a strange sort of way. I'm going to have a closer look.'

He leapt enthusiastically out of the Land Rover and walked as if drawn by a magnet across the dusty eucalyptus grove to the foot of the vast megalith.

Charles felt the twentieth century slipping away. With every footstep he journeyed into the past, into a world of cosmic consciousness, a world free from pop music, glass skyscrapers, inner-city deprivation, and drunken men watching television. Here in Packer's Creek in the immensity of the outback a man could truly find his soul.

His meditation was disturbed by sounds coming from the other side of the rock, seeming vaguely familiar. Was it the didgeridoo summoning up the spirit of Donga for a feast? Perhaps some sort of marriage ritual involving the tribal dancing of the Bella Moonies? His pace quickened and, turning the corner, he came upon a tin hut bearing the legend 'Welcome to Boolabanga Aboriginal Craft Centre and Beer Tent'.

Of crafts, however, there was no trace and the ground outside was littered with rusting beer cans. From the darkened interior of the hut came the sound of girlish laughter mingled with the familiar strains of Michael Jackson's *Bad*. Charles wearily opened the door to find his wife gyrating delightedly with a number of small dark half-naked men to the sounds emanating from a new video recorder.

'Come in, sport!' cried one grizzled old dancer. 'And grab yourself a tinny. There's plenty in the fridge.'

Diana's shrill voice joined in. 'Darling, you were right! These abos are absolutely wonderful!' The men roared appreciatively.

Outside through the dusty window of the hut Charles could see the shadow of the great rock falling across the blighted landscape of his dreams . . .

♛ *Chapter 14* ♛

Charles and Diana have returned from Australia refreshed by their experience and hoping to embark on a new chapter in their relationship.

THE EVENINGS were already getting lighter, Charles noticed as the Tomkinson clock struck five. From his seat by the window he could see the first crocuses thrusting their gaily coloured trumpets through the icy sod, a harbinger of spring. Charles felt a surge of hope course through his veins, and began to hum along with the music of the repeat of *This Week's Composer* on Radio 3. The baroque strains of Thomasino Frescobaldi filled the room with lightness and merriment.

Charles dabbed a bright yellow blob of paint on his canvas to represent the sun setting over Castlemaine Rock, the great outcrop in the Australian outback. His new picture, which he had provisionally entitled *Songline of the Dreamer*, was coming along well. It seemed to glow with the same spirit as the happy tribal warriors of the Pilgers he had met.

What a tremendously exciting journey it had been! A terrific exploration of all sorts of things. And how much Diana had benefited, he thought – she had sort of blossomed in the heat. A montage of memories was thrown up in his mind: the Tall Ships sailing in the harbour; he and Diana boogie-woogieing to the music of the Sydney Harbour Moonlight Serenaders; playing the cello, to the delight of the jovial pressmen; and, to cap it all, Diana's triumphant performance of Rachmaninov's *Chopsticks*.

'Music is indeed the Food of Love,' he mused as he laid down his brush, elated by the creative effort. He got up and stepped back to observe his handiwork. The solitary rock reminded him of the words of his friend and mentor, Sir Laurens van der Post: 'At the centre of each life there is a great rock, which we must climb if we are to see beyond the horizon.' How very true that was. He resolved there and then to present the picture to his friend.

The radio announcer broke into his reverie. 'On Radio 3 this evening we are to hear the first performance of a new work by Alain Yentobbe.'

Yes! Music. That was the answer. It was music that had brought them together in Australia. It would work the same magic in the quiet setting of their Gloucestershire home.

*T*o his delight, Diana had responded warmly to his suggestion of a musical evening. 'Brill! That would be a blast!' she had exclaimed, and at once had volunteered to organize the whole thing.

Now Charles took his cherished old cello, an original Mantovani, a present from King Faht of Saudi Arabia, from underneath the bed where it had lain gathering dust for many years. As he turned it, the mellow instrument responded to his warm caress. It would all come flooding back to him, he felt sure, once he had got – how could he put it? – 'In the Mood'. And, sure enough, from below could he not hear the strains of his young accompanist warming up on the piano? But the tune was unfamiliar and the rhythm insistent and strangely drum-like.

Clutching the cello, Charles hurried downstairs to the drawing room and threw open the door.

The room was in darkness, save for a set of flashing stroboscopic devices which illuminated in turn the perspiring and excited faces

- GARY ANDREWS 1988 -

of Bunty Coker, Charlie Ricketson-Smythe, Georgie Cavendish and Duchess Fergiana, who was defying the doctor's advice and gyrating to the music emanating from two giant speakers perched precariously on the priceless seventeenth-century Parkinson dresser.

And there was Diana behind a set of turntables, standing next to a tall animated Caribbean figure dressed in a gold leather tuxedo, his hair dyed an exotic shade of turquoise.

'Play this one, J.J.,' she giggled. 'This one's really great. Listen everyone – J.J.'s putting on Michael Jackson's *Bad*!'

The guests cheered delightedly.

'Amazing!'

'Fab!'

Charles closed the door quietly and walked solemnly back to his room. He would be in time for the concert from Vienna. The bleak strains of Yentobbe would match his mood precisely. If music be the food of love, then surely he was starving . . .

👑 *Chapter 15* 👑

'PASS THE PORT, old boy . . . No, no, the other way, Mr Wilson.' Everyone sniggered as the editor of *The Times* sent the exquisite Waterstone decanter in the wrong direction.

However, they all seemed to be getting on well, Charles thought as he surveyed the celebrated dignitaries he had assembled from the superior end of Fleet Street.

There they were, all in full evening dress apart from Mr Wilson, who had come straight from the office in his green eyeshade and shirt sleeves. To his left sat Pennington Wellington, editor of the *Economist*; next to him, Mr Andreas Whittam-Strobes, the legendary founder of the Newspaper of the Year, the one that Charles read to Diana over breakfast each morning. But perhaps the most impressive of all the guests at his table was the silver-haired doyen of Fleet Street, Sir Peregrine Worsthorne, resplendent in a superbly tailored maroon velveteen dinner suit, his many decorations glittering on his lapels.

'Take my word for it, Sir,' said Perry, as Charles was now calling him, drawing him discreetly to one side. 'It would be quite wrong of you to judge our profession by the antics of the gutter press.'

Charles agreed. 'Some of the things they've said about Diana and one's self are simply amazing, pure make-believe.'

Sir Peregrine's wise old head nodded earnestly. 'Appalling, Sir. Quite appalling.'

At the other end of the table a chorus of raucous laughter greeted

yet another of Mr Wilson's racing anecdotes recounted in his colourful Glaswegian dialect.

Sir Peregrine gestured disapprovingly at them. 'I would like you to think, Sir, that there are those of us in whom you may confide at any time with complete confidence.' He pulled on his cigar. 'Tell me, Sir, what is really on your mind?'

And out it all came. Charles opened his heart to the benign Sir Peregrine. For once the expression 'a gentleman of the press' seemed appropriate. It reminded him of other occasions deep in the Kalahari bush where, by the embers of the camp fire, he had bared his soul to another white-haired sage, his old friend and mentor, Sir Laurens van der Post. As he had put it, 'A man who opens the door to his heart will never be locked within it.'

Long after the footmen had helped Mr Wilson to his car, Charles and Perry were still deep in conversation, the younger man talking and the older man hanging intently on every word . . .

♕　　　　♕　　　　♕

*T*he Duke of Edinburgh burst through the mahogany door of the elegant breakfast room at Windsor Castle. He was clutching the morning papers, his face purple, the veins standing out on his forehead like the tightened rigging of a clipper in full sail.

'What the bloody hell is this?' he roared. And there they were again, the screaming headlines:

' "My Secret Torment" by Prince Charles.' ' "I Wanna Be Bob Geldof!" says Loopy Prince.' ' "Why I Ban Di's Can" by His Royal Looniness.' And that was only the *Telegraph*. *The Times*, the *Independent* and the *Guardian* all followed suit.

As Charles read with horror through one story after another, his heart pounded with an overwhelming sense of betrayal. All of his most intimate thoughts were splashed for the world to see after he had been assured that he was entering into a sacred confidence, one that would never be disclosed to a living soul.

The Duke towered over his son, just as Herr Waldheim, the sadistic PT instructor at Gordonstoun, had so often done in the dark days of Charles's youth.

'I thought you'd learnt your lesson, you little fool. Never talk to these press johnnies. They're all the bloody same.'

Charles knew it would be impossible to explain to his father just how he had been betrayed, but more impossible to explain that what his father had read was indeed true. Yes! To be of value. To be of use. To be like Geldof – that would really be something.

'And what's this about bloody Geldof? Fellow can't even shave properly. Your mother nearly had a fit when she had to pin a gong on him. Can't open his bloody mouth without swearing.'

Charles cringed. It was a waste of time arguing with his father.

The Duke turned on his heels and strode from the room. 'If you're bored, young man, there's plenty of wildlife to be shot. That'll keep you busy.'

He slammed the door behind him. Charles felt terribly alone, more isolated than ever before. Was there no one at all he could trust? In his mind he could picture the silvery-haired Sir Peregrine guffawing with his cronies in some club as he regaled them with Charles's innermost thoughts.

'Encore un rêve disparu,' he thought as he stared into the cold uneaten boiled egg congealing before him . . .

Chapter 16

Charles has gone to America to deliver a series of lectures at the prestigious Pittsburgh Institute of Architecture, leaving his young wife Diana alone at Highgrove.

CHARLES SAT at the end of his king-size bed and looked at his watch. It would be too early to ring Diana. He would give it another hour and she would be there as she had promised.

He was eager to tell her about his speech that evening, 'The Spirit of the Past Living in the Present', which had gone down so well.

Four hundred thousand of America's leading architects had flown in especially for the convention and sat attentively in the Schwarzenegger Foundation as he developed his theme about what he had called 'the modernistic conspiracy in which the ordinary individual is alienated by huge towers of concrete and glass'.

And what a perfect place to say it, he thought disconsolately as he crossed to the window and stared at the jungle of skyscrapers crowding menacingly around him.

And yet, as so often in the New World, there had been a sympathetic ear for his message. After his speech the doyen of American architects, Milo di Gropius II, had shambled up to him and put an affectionate arm around his shoulders.

'You socked it to 'em real good, Charlie baby. Enjoy.'

Yes, that would really be something to tell Diana. It wouldn't be long now before the time they had arranged for their telephonic tryst across the Atlantic.

But how to fill in the grey hour that stretched ahead of him in the specially furbished Royal Suite on the 83rd floor of the Pittsburgh Sinatra Hotel?

Suddenly he felt alone. A terrible sense of isolation gripped him, a stranger in this city of strangers. Even the message of his old friend and mentor, Sir Laurens van der Post – 'No man is ever truly alone when he has his own soul to walk beside him' – failed to give him solace. The words rang hollow somehow. It was a human voice that he needed. What matter if Diana was indifferent to his vision of the ideal city? At least she would be there. Just to say 'hello' would be enough . . .

Charles switched on the giant 78-inch 24-channel television set built into the fridge at the foot of his bed. To his amazement, he was greeted by the sight of his brother Andrew and the Duchess Fergiana going down the Mississippi on a paddle-steamer. He listened carefully to the commentary . . .

'And here's King Andrew and his young queen, the lovely Princess Diana, entering into the spirit of things dressed as a bar-girl from the Old Kentucky Horseshoe Saloon Bar. Howdy your Royal Pardners! Have a nice day!'

In irritation he changed channels, only to find his sister-in-law dressed as a Red Indian, her long red hair cascading down her back in a bizarre arrangement of plaits, with a Cabbage Patch doll papoose strapped around her neck.

'Your place or mine?' she leered provocatively at Big Chief Samuel Jacobovitz, the Mayor of Lake Woebegon, Colorado.

Horrified by what he felt to be the sheer vulgarity of Andrew's wife, he could not help thinking how very differently his own Diana had behaved in similar circumstances. How serene, how regal, how beautiful . . .

He tried another channel. And another. But there she was again. Fergie laughing. Fergie dancing. Fergie the centre of attraction.

Defeated, he watched mesmerized as she told the Seattle Windsurfers' Association a joke about a black bishop and a can-can dancer that Charles had heard many times from the lips of his father.

The phone rang, the single beep of the American system that he so admired. At last! He snatched up the receiver.

'We're putting you through now, Mr Prince,' said the honeyed voice of the operator. 'Enjoy your call.'

There was a series of clicks and then the familiar purr of the Highgrove telephone. He could picture the old black Bakelite receiver, designed by Sir Gavin de Stamp, sitting on the ornate sixteenth-century Roccoforte hall table. It would take Diana only a few seconds to hear and answer it. He imagined her hurrying down the corridor, her long legs striding out like a young gazelle across the priceless Shakoorana carpet.

And still the phone rang. Ten times . . . Twenty times . . . Thirty times . . . And still it rang. Charles's heart started to pound. What could have happened?

From the corner of his eye he could see the mocking figure of Princess Fergiana dancing with a giant Mickey Mouse made of ice-cream.

Where was she? Diana . . . Diana . . .

And then, at last, just as he had decided to replace the handset, there came an answer.

'No, Your Highness. It's Mrs Frimble speaking. I'm afraid she's gone to London.' The broad Gloucestershire brogue of his faithful housekeeper came, crystal clear, across 2,000 miles.

'The gentlemen called for her in the car earlier on, Sir. A Mr Ricketson-Smythe and a Mr Bunty Coker, I believe. No, Sir, nothing about a phone call. She said she didn't know when she'd be back.'

Charles hung up and looked out at the Pittsburgh skyline. A million electric lights twinkled their message of mockery, a million laughing eyes set deep in the dark, sullen blackness . . .

♛ *Chapter 17* ♛

Charles is searching for a role, and feels more and more that the world he is to inherit must be a world free of man's foolishness.

SOMETHING WAS odd. What was it? Pall Mall empty of cars? Charles crossed the normally busy street and entered St James's Park. The trill of birdsong filled the air and all around him was the sound of happy laughter. Where was the traffic noise at 12.00 on a workday Friday? Surely he had not forgotten a state visit, for heaven's sake?

A small blue-eared Caledonian squirrel, the variety which he knew faced certain extinction, ran happily over his shoe towards a nest bursting with hoarded nuts. Wherever he looked there were flowers of every conceivable variety – the friendly pinks and yellows of the Weidenfeld Lilies, the gay oranges and violets of the Dumpster Daisies, the noble reds of the Abbey National Roses. And wasn't that a brass band playing merrily by the lake, to the obvious delight of the puffins and flamingos? Yes, it was a medley from Andrew Lloyd Webber's *Cats*.

Charles whistled as he strolled towards Trafalgar Square. Curiouser and curiouser, he mused. The buildings that lined Whitehall and the Haymarket, once so grey and drab, now sparkled white in the spring sunshine. Here and there cyclists waved at him as they silently journeyed to their jolly destinations.

And something else was missing. Where were those hideous monstrosities of glass and concrete that he had so often railed against in conference halls throughout the world? As if by some sort of science fiction thing, Charles thought, some kind of Spielberg effect like that film that Diana had so much enjoyed, the modern buildings had all gone.

And where was Diana, his lovely young wife, with her pale-blue eyes and blushing cheeks? How extraordinary! Even as he spoke her name, so she appeared, dressed in the manner of a comely country wench, and instead of a Walkman she carried a yoke with pails of fresh cream. So there were cows in London. It was incredible!

Diana smiled bewitchingly and took his arm. 'I want to show you something,' she said, leading him down to the river where young children bathed in the pure waters of the Thames. Large dolphins

leapt playfully in the blue, and there was his brother on a surfboard, gliding on a gentle wave under Hungerford Bridge. And on the bank was the sprightly figure of Sir Hugh Casson, his straw hat at a rakish angle on his head, as he sketched in watercolours, capturing the enchanting prospect before him. A group of windmills clustering by the bank – surely once the site of that ghastly National Theatre; Colditz-on-Thames, as he had once wittily described it in a speech – met his view.

It was then that Diana gestured towards the city. 'Look, Your Majesty,' she said. 'They've carried out your orders to the letter!' His eyes followed the line of her pointing finger.

There stood the great dome of St Paul's as it had in the days of yore. The vast cupola towered over the tiny cottages and tenements nestling beneath its benevolent shadow. Smoke curled from a hundred thatched chimneys into the azure blue sky as powerfully built blacksmiths hammered on the anvils of a hundred workshops. And here came Sir John Betjeman on a white shire horse, his quill poised above the parchment on which he was putting the finishing touches to a poem that summed up the feelings of all noble yeomen of England.

'Hail Charles! Hail King Charles, the Saviour of the Race! Yes, we salute you! All hail!' As the venerable bard recited the words they were lost beneath the peal of ancient bells triumphantly ringing louder . . . louder . . . louder . . .

Charles woke with a start. The nineteenth-century Thomas Telford carriage clock chimed four. He shook his head and, as the vision faded, Charles realized with immense sadness that it had all been a dream and he was still sitting in his favourite Parker Bowles leather armchair in his study. The notes of his speech to the Euro-Heritage Young Environmentalist Awards of 1988 dinner lay scattered before him.

The words of his old friend and mentor, Sir Laurens van der Post, welled up unbidden from that inner self. 'If a man dreams that he is a butterfly then he may wake up to discover that he is only a caterpillar.' How true, how very, very true . . .

♛ *Chapter 18* ♛

It is Charles's 40th birthday. Will it mark a turning point for him, or must he remain the Heir of Sorrows?

THE AUTUMN leaves lay like a gold-brown carpet across the green sward of Highgrove Park as two figures strode out bracing themselves against the chill morning air. Sir Laurens van der Post, an erect nonagenarian, paused and leant on his stick, a gift from the Massai warriors of Bananarama. He looked up at the grey sky and gestured towards a solitary lapwing hovering above the branches of a yellowing beech tree.

'It is the time of the changing,' Sir Laurens told his young friend. 'The season when the Jojoba Bushmen set out on their long journey to their winter pastures. And so it is with all of us,' he said, looking pointedly at Charles. The Prince nodded as the two men continued their walk along the Von Reibnitz mile, down the long avenue of majestic oaks which had withstood the hurricanes of centuries.

'Yes,' the old sage continued. 'Forty is a milestone placed on the brow of every man's hill when we pause and look backward, but then look forward to the road ahead and where it might lead.'

'Yes, that's tremendously fascinating,' Charles said mechanically, but as he looked back at his own road he could only see frustration, half-finished projects, half-fulfilled dreams. And ahead? A mist descended and he could see no landmark to guide him. He suddenly felt uncomfortable and told the old man of his doubts and fears.

Sir Laurens paused and in his old eyes glowed the embers of profound wisdom. 'Yes,' said the sage. 'Yes, yes, I see.'

♛　　　　♛　　　　♛

Charles sat in the magnificent fourteenth-century Jacobean marble bath, which his cousin David Hicks had found in an antique dealer's off the Portobello Road. The soapy water had long gone cold and Charles sat there, growing more gloomy by the minute as he contemplated the evening.

'Leave it to me,' Diana had said. 'I want it to be a surprise.' He knew what her surprises meant. The sponge drifted damp and cold towards him and lodged against his chest. He could picture the scene that evening vividly.

The usual gang were sure to be there. Charlie Ricketson-Smythe, with his awful jokes, chain-smoking and drinking vodka. Georgie Cavendish braying with laughter like some hideous creature from the zoo. Bunty Coker trying to borrow money. And to top it all his brother and the awful Fergiana. No doubt she would come looking like Edna Everage as usual.

As Charles climbed out and wrapped the Irish linen towel around him he sighed and gazed into the antique Louis Armstrong mirror. With his finger he traced the figures 4,0 in the condensation and watched disconsolately as his face revealed itself in the clearing glass.

'Life begins at 40,' they said. To him it seemed little more than a cruel joke. He tried to recall what Sir Laurens had said that morning but try as he might he could not.

👑   👑   👑

*D*iana was waiting for him downstairs. She looked more beautiful than ever in a black Hirohito crêpe-de-chine off-the-shoulder mini-skirt. He felt his heart leap as she took his arm and ushered him into the darkened dining room.

'Close your eyes,' Diana said playfully. 'I'm going to turn on the light.' Charles knew what was coming. But when he opened his eyes he could scarcely believe what he saw.

In the middle of the room was a table set for two. Candles burnt brightly in ornate silver Otto Beuselinck holders, whilst a single red rose graced a priceless Trelford cut-crystal vase on the polished table.

'A table for two,' she whispered as she bent down to switch on the record player. The exquisite strains of Lloyd Webber's *Requiem*, his current favourite, filled the room and there at his place was his own latest painting of their holiday in El Palazzio di Bertorelli, in Minorca, as guests of his cousin Ferdinand the Brave, now magnificently framed. It was adorned with a simple message, the three words that throughout history have meant so much to so many.

There was a discreet pop as Sir Alan Fitztightly opened the champagne, poured two sparkling glasses and offered them to the couple. Shyly Diana raised her glass and clinked it against his.

For the first time in what seemed like an eternity he felt an incredible lightness. For years in the wildernesses of the world, in the heat of the desert and the icy cool of the mountains he had been searching . . . and yet all the time the answer had been there. The key to his happiness was by his side, leaning towards him, her glass upraised.

'Happy birthday, darling,' she said, placing an affectionate kiss on his cheek. The mists cleared, his fears dispersed, the way forward beckoned.

👑   👑   👑

*W*as it his imagination or could he at that very moment hear the sound of Bunty Coker's BMW crunching the gravel in the drive outside? Was it his imagination . . .?

FOR THE BEST IN PAPERBACKS, LOOK FOR THE 🐧

In every corner of the world, on every subject under the sun, Penguin represents quality and variety – the very best in publishing today.

For complete information about books available from Penguin – including Pelicans, Puffins, Peregrines and Penguin Classics – and how to order them, write to us at the appropriate address below. Please note that for copyright reasons the selection of books varies from country to country.

In the United Kingdom: For a complete list of books available from Penguin in the U.K., please write to *Dept E.P., Penguin Books Ltd, Harmondsworth, Middlesex, UB7 0DA*

In the United States: For a complete list of books available from Penguin in the U.S., please write to *Dept BA, Penguin, 299 Murray Hill Parkway, East Rutherford, New Jersey 07073*

In Canada: For a complete list of books available from Penguin in Canada, please write to *Penguin Books Canada Ltd, 2801 John Street, Markham, Ontario L3R 1B4*

In Australia: For a complete list of books available from Penguin in Australia, please write to the *Marketing Department, Penguin Books Australia Ltd, P.O. Box 257, Ringwood, Victoria 3134*

In New Zealand: For a complete list of books available from Penguin in New Zealand, please write to the *Marketing Department, Penguin Books (NZ) Ltd, Private Bag, Takapuna, Auckland 9*

In India: For a complete list of books available from Penguin, please write to *Penguin Overseas Ltd, 706 Eros Apartments, 56 Nehru Place, New Delhi, 110019*

In Holland: For a complete list of books available from Penguin in Holland, please write to *Penguin Books Nederland B.V., Postbus 195, NL–1380AD Weesp, Netherlands*

In Germany: For a complete list of books available from Penguin, please write to *Penguin Books Ltd, Friedrichstrasse 10 – 12, D–6000 Frankfurt Main 1, Federal Republic of Germany*

In Spain: For a complete list of books available from Penguin in Spain, please write to *Longman Penguin España, Calle San Nicolas 15, E–28013 Madrid, Spain*

FOR THE BEST IN PAPERBACKS, LOOK FOR THE

PENGUIN BESTSELLERS

Is That It? Bob Geldof with Paul Vallely

The autobiography of one of today's most controversial figures. 'He has become a folk hero whom politicians cannot afford to ignore. And he has shown that simple moral outrage can be a force for good' – *Daily Telegraph*. 'It's terrific . . . everyone over thirteen should read it' – *Standard*

Niccolò Rising Dorothy Dunnett

The first of a new series of historical novels by the author of the world-famous *Lymond* series. Adventure, high romance and the danger-ous glitter of fifteenth-century Europe abound in this magnificent story of the House of Charetty and the disarming, mysterious genius who exploits all its members.

The World, the Flesh and the Devil Reay Tannahill

'A bewitching blend of history and passion. A MUST' – *Daily Mail*. A superb novel in a great tradition. 'Excellent' – *The Times*

Perfume: The Story of a Murderer Patrick Süskind

It was after his first murder that Grenouille knew he was a genius. He was to become the greatest perfumer of all time, for he possessed the power to distil the very essence of love itself. 'Witty, stylish and ferociously absorbing . . . menace conveyed with all the power of the writer's elegant unease' – *Observer*

The Old Devils Kingsley Amis

Winner of the 1986 Booker Prize
'Vintage Kingsley Amis, 50 per cent pure alcohol with splashes of sad savagery' – *The Times*. The highly comic novel about Alun Weaver and his wife's return to their Celtic roots. 'Crackling with marvellous Taff comedy . . . this is probably Mr Amis's best book since *Lucky Jim*' – *Guardian*

FOR THE BEST IN PAPERBACKS, LOOK FOR THE

PENGUIN BESTSELLERS

Cat Chaser Elmore Leonard

'*Cat Chaser* really moves' – *The New York Times Book Review*. 'Elmore Leonard gets so much mileage out of his plot that just when you think one is cruising to a stop, it picks up speed for a few more twists and turns' – *Washington Post*.

Men and Angels Mary Gordon

A rich, astonishing novel of the limits of human and divine love.' A domestic drama of morals with a horrifying climax . . . compellingly readable' – *Sunday Times*. 'A brilliant study of the insatiable demands of the unlovable' – *Standard*

The Mosquito Coast Paul Theroux

Detesting twentieth century America, Allie Fox takes his family to live in the Honduran jungle. 'Imagine the Swiss Family Robinson gone mad, and you will have some idea of what is in store . . . Theroux's best novel yet' – *Sunday Times* (Now a powerful film.)

The King's Garden Fanny Deschamps

In a story which ranges from the opulent corruption of Louis XV's court to the storms and dangers of life on the high seas, Jeanne pursues her happiness and the goal of true love with all the determination and his spirits of one born to succeed . . .

Let No Man Divide Elizabeth Kary

Set against the turmoil of the American Civil War, *Let No Man Divide* tells of Leigh Pemberton's desire to nurse the wounded and live an independent life, and her secret yearning for Hayes Bannister, the man who has saved her life and taken her breath away.

FOR THE BEST IN PAPERBACKS, LOOK FOR THE

PENGUIN BESTSELLERS

Castaway   Lucy Irvine

'A savagely self-searching tale . . . she is a born writer as well as a ruthlessly talented survivor' – *Observer*. 'Fascinating' – *Daily Mail*. 'Remarkable . . . such dreams as stuff is made of' – *Financial Times*

Runaway   Lucy Irvine

Not a sequel, but the story of Lucy Irvine's life *before* she became a castaway. Witty, courageous and sensational, it is a story you won't forget. 'A searing account . . . raw and unflinching honesty' – *Daily Express*. 'A genuine and courageous work of autobiography' – *Today*

The Adventures of Goodnight and Loving   Leslie Thomas

Sometimes touching, sometimes hilarious, sometimes alarming, the adventures of George Goodnight represent a quest for excitement and love. 'A constant pleasure. Leslie Thomas is to the contemporary novel what Alan Ayckborn is to the Theatre: a wry humorist with the rare ability to make his audience feel as well as laugh' – *Sunday Telegraph*

Wideacre   Philippa Gregory

Beatrice Lacey is one of the most passionate and compelling heroines ever created. There burns in Beatrice one overwhelming obsession – to possess Wideacre, her family's ancestral home, and to achieve her aim she will risk everything; reputation, incest, even murder.

A Dark and Distant Shore   Reay Tannahill

'An absorbing saga spanning a century of love affairs, hatred and high-points of Victorian history' – *Daily Express*. 'Enthralling . . . a marvellous blend of *Gone with the Wind* and *The Thorn Birds*. You will enjoy every page' – *Daily Mirror*

FOR THE BEST IN PAPERBACKS, LOOK FOR THE

PENGUIN BESTSELLERS

Goodbye Soldier   Spike Milligan

The final volume of his war memoirs in which we find Spike in Italy, in civvies and in love with a beautiful ballerina. 'Desperately funny, vivid, vulgar' – *Sunday Times*

The Nudists   Guy Bellamy

Simon Venables, honeymooning under the scorching sun, has just seen the woman he should have married . . . 'It is rare for a book to be comic, happy and readable all at once, but Guy Bellamy's *The Nudists* is just that' – *Daily Telegraph*. 'Funny caustic and gloriously readable' – *London Standard*

I, Tina   Tina Turner with Kurt Loder

'Tina Turner . . . has achieved the impossible; not one but two legends in her own lifetime' – *Cosmopolitan*. *I, Tina* tells the astonishing story that lies behind her success; electrifying, moving and unforgettable, it is one of the great life stories in rock-music history.

A Dark-Adapted Eye   Barbara Vine

Writing as Barbara Vine, Ruth Rendell has created a labyrinthine journey into the heart of the Hillyard family, living in the respectable middle-class countryside after the Second World War. 'Barbara Vine has the kind of near-Victorian narrative drive that compels a reader to go on turning the pages' – Julian Symons in the *Sunday Times*

Survive!   John Man

Jan Little, with her husband and daughter, escaped to the depths of the Brazilian jungle. Only she survived. Almost blind and totally alone, Jan Little triumphed over death, horror and desolation. Hers is a story of remarkable courage and tenacity.

A Man Made to Measure   Elaine Crowley

Set in Dublin during the First World War, the story of *A Man Made to Measure* follows the fortunes of a group of people whose lives are changed forever by the fateful events of the Easter Uprising. 'Elaine Crowley writes like a dream . . . an exciting new discovery' – *Annabel*

FOR THE BEST IN PAPERBACKS, LOOK FOR THE 🐧

PENGUIN BESTSELLERS

Relative Strangers   Maureen Rissik

Angie Wyatt has three enviable assets: money, beauty and a tenacious instinct for survival. She is a woman fighting for success in a complex world of ambition and corruption. '*Relative Strangers* is a wonderful, intelligently written novel – a pleasure to read' – Susan Isaacs, author of *Compromising Positions*

O-Zone   Paul Theroux

It's New Year in paranoid, computer-rich New York, and a group of Owners has jet-rotored out to party in O-Zone, the radioactive wasteland where the people do not officially exist. 'Extremely exciting . . . as ferocious and as well-written as *The Mosquito Coast*, and that's saying something' – *The Times*

Time/Steps   Charlotte Vale Allen

Beatrice Crane was the little girl from Toronto with magic feet and driving talent. She was going to be a star. It was more important to her than her family, than friendship or other people's rules . . . more important, even than love.

Blood Red Rose   Maxwell Grant

China 1926. As Communist opposition to the oppressive Nationalist army grows, this vast and ancient country draws nearer to the brink of a devastating civil war. As Kate Richmond is drawn into the struggle, her destiny becomes irrevocably entwined with the passions of a divided China and her ideals and her love are tested to the utmost.

Cry Freedom   John Briley

Written by award-winning scriptwriter John Briley, this is the book of Richard Attenborough's powerful new film of the same name. Beginning with Donald Woods's first encounter with Steve Biko, it follows their friendship, their political activism and their determination to fight minority rule to Steve Biko's death and Woods's dramatic escape. It is both a thrilling adventure and a bold political statement.

FOR THE BEST IN PAPERBACKS, LOOK FOR THE 🐧

PENGUIN OMNIBUSES

Life with Jeeves   P. G. Wodehouse

Containing *Right Ho, Jeeves*, *The Inimitable Jeeves* and *Very Good, Jeeves!*, this is a delicious collection of vintage Wodehouse in which the old master lures us, once again, into the evergreen world of Bertie Wooster, his terrifying Aunt Agatha, and, of course, the inimitable Jeeves.

Perfick! Perfick!   H. E. Bates

The adventures of the irrepressible Larkin family, in four novels: *The Darling Buds of May*, *A Breath of French Air*, *When the Green Woods Laugh* and *Oh! To Be in England*.

The Best of Modern Humour   Edited by Mordecai Richler

Packed between the covers of this book is the teeming genius of modern humour's foremost exponents from both sides of the Atlantic – and for every conceivable taste. Here is everyone from Tom Wolfe, S. J. Perelman, John Mortimer, Alan Coren, Woody Allen, John Berger and Fran Lebowitz to P. G. Wodehouse, James Thurber and Evelyn Waugh.

Enderby   Anthony Burgess

'These three novels are the richest and most verbally dazzling comedies Burgess has written' – *Listener*. Containing the three volumes *Inside Enderby*, *Enderby Outside* and *The Clockwork Treatment*.

Vintage Thurber: Vol. One   James Thurber

A selection of his best writings and drawings, this *grand-cru* volume includes *Let Your Mind Alone*, *My World and Welcome to It*, *Fables for Our Time*, *Famous Poems Illustrated*, *Men, Women and Dogs*, *The Beast in Me* and *Thurber Country* – as well as much, much more.

Vintage Thurber: Vol. Two   James Thurber

'Without question America's foremost humorist' – *The Times Literary Supplement*. In this volume, where vintage piles upon vintage, are *The Middle-aged Man on the Flying Trapeze*, *The Last Flower*, *My Life and Hard Times*, *The Owl in the Attic*, *The Seal in the Bedroom* and *The Thurber Carnival*.